WHEN THE HURT... STOPS HURTING

INITA ELLIOTT MCLUCAS

CANDACE JOYNER
PUBLISHING

Copyright © 2023 by INITA Elliott McLucas
When The Hurt... Stops Hurting

ISBN 978-1-7375902-2-4

Printed in the United States of America

All rights reserved solely by the Author; this book or parts thereof may not be reproduced in any form by any means, mechanical, graphic, screenshots, photocopying, scanning, digitizing, taping, web distribution, information networks or information storage, retrieval systems, and electronic, except as permitted under section 107 or 108 of the 1976 United States Copyright Act, without the prior written permission of the Author.
Scriptures marked KJV are taken from the King James Version

This book recounts events in the life of Inita Elliott McLucas according to the author's recollection and perspective. While all stories are true, some names and identifying details have been changed to protect the privacy of those involved.

Candace Joyner Publishing
P. O. Box 310
Lumberton, NC 28359
www.candacejoyner.com

When The Hurt... Stops Hurting /Inita Eliott McLucas

Foreword

I have known the author, Inita McLucas, since high school over forty-six years ago. It is an honor and privilege to write these words. I did not know her back in high school the same way I got to know her years later. I came to know her as a woman of God, strong in her faith. I have seen her go through and endure many hardships that only God himself could have brought her through. One thing I do know is that God allows bad things to happen to good people for a reason. And in this book, I am sure you will find that out. I was so excited about this book. I don't know everything she has been through, but I do know she kept the Faith and Hope alive. Congratulations! To God be the Glory.

Stella A. Burns

Acknowledgments

First, I give all Glory and Honor to my Lord and Savior Jesus Christ, for allowing me to write this book.

I acknowledge my supportive husband Glenn, who did not mind me telling my story.

We have three handsome sons, Murrell, Terrellis, Durrellis and another son we helped raise, named Calvin.

We also have three beautiful daughters that we've raised, Teresa, Initsha and Shante'. Glenn and I also have three beautiful daughters-in-love, Aurelia, Stephanie, and Lizzy. We have fourteen grandchildren, too many to name (LOL) a little great-grandson, and two more great-grandchildren on the way.

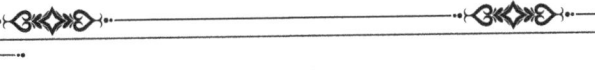

I would be remiss if I did not acknowledge my Uncle Jr. (Pops) and Aunt Ruther Jane (mom) for raising me from fifth grade until I was grown and married. I thank you two because you did not have to do it.

And I certainly cannot leave out my Pastor, James Powell and First Lady Jackie Powell along with my entire Abundant Grace Church Family.

Dedication

I would like to dedicate this book to Elizabeth Elliott (Mother). She was my grandmother, but we all called her "Mother." She took me in and raised me from an infant until I was in the fifth grade. I wish she was here to see What God has done through a little poor girl from Wade, NC. But God can do what seems impossible. "Thank you, Jesus."

I also would like to dedicate this book to a dear friend and client, Doretha Rawls. She was indeed a prayer warrior. I know she would be so proud of me. I miss you, "Doe."

And I certainly cannot leave out my niece Kimberly McLean. She would be so proud of her Aunt Nita. Always encouraging others and had a saying, "Look what God did," "That lil' girl from Wade," and "Who would have thought?"

Table of Contents

Preface 1

1. "WHEN THE HURT STOPS HURTING" 3
2. "HOW IS LIFE LIVING IN NEW YORK?" 5
3. "HURTING THEN BUT DIDN'T UNDERSTAND" 6
4. "A RING" 8
5. "RECORD PLAYER" 9
6. "GOING TO HIGH SCHOOL" 11
7. "HOW I MET MY HUSBAND" 12
8. "I PLANNED TO KILL THEM BOTH" 15
9. "GOD INTERVENES THROUGH A SONG" 17
10. "GENE COMES IN FROM BASIC TRAINING" 20
11. "THINGS ARE STARTING TO CHANGE" 23
12. "WHEN THE REAL HURT BEGINS" 24
13. "RECEIVING THAT PRECIOUS GIFT OF THE HOLY GHOST" 32
14. "THINGS WERE LOOKING A LITTLE BETTER" 37
15. "I PAID MY TITHES" 39
16. "THANKFUL FOR MY CHURCH FAMILY" 41
17. "GOD WILL DELIVER, EVENTUALLY" 43

Preface

I am writing this book because my life had so many turns. From birth, when my birth mother gave me away at only one month old. I grew up poor with my grandparents, who were raising me along with eleven other children and grandchildren together. Falling in love with a man that just took my weakness for granted. Hurting me and hurting me until one day I got sick and tired.

I finally learned that there was and is a man that would love me in spite of His name -- Jesus.

I think the testimony of my life will encourage hurt ladies that God can and will deliver. That day will come when the Hurt Stops Hurting!

You must read the next two additions to find out exactly when my Hurt Stopped Hurting!

1
"WHEN THE HURT STOPS HURTING"

It takes the Lord to take the hurt away. I was born in Brooklyn, New York to Maggie. Being only one month old, I was given away and brought to live and be raised by my grandparents, Lizzie, and James Elliott in the small town of Wade, North Carolina.

There, in this small home, lived eleven children and the grandparents with a total of thirteen people living in this small 3-bedroom house. I did not know anything about God growing up, nor was I raised going to church. I did not hear anything about God unless it was in a curse word. But Mother and Daddy did the best they could. We did not eat what we wanted, but we had food. I don't ever remember going days without food, so I guess we did not go hungry.

Well, as life goes on Daddy died in 1968 of May. I remember going to the funeral. At this time, I was at the end of third grade, about to go to fourth grade. We never went to church, so this was the first time that I had ever been in a church for any reason.

I remember the funeral was at this church in Wade. I assume the family was fairly large because I remember sitting closer to the back of the church. I still remember the song that the choir sang, even though it was my first time ever in a church, hearing gospel music or a preacher preach.

Even to this day, I remember the words to the song. The song was, "You've gotta move, you've gotta move, you've gotta move, you've gotta move, cause when the Lord, the Lord gets ready you gotta to move. You may be high, you may be low, you may be rich, you may be poor, but when the Lord, the Lord gets ready you've gotta move."

I was just a little child, and now a grown lady, and remember as if it was just a few years ago. I remember a feeling that I felt, not knowing what the feeling was. It was not a feeling that daddy was gone, because I did not understand death anyway. I realized after I was saved and Holy Ghost filled with the evidence of speaking in tongues, "as the spirit of God gave utterance" (Acts 2:4). That it was the presence of God.

2

"HOW IS LIFE LIVING IN NEW YORK?"

By and by Mother found a better house for us still in Wade, but it was better than what we had. By this time, I was in the fourth grade and would sometimes think about my birth mother. I didn't know much about her because she was living in New York with her two other kids and her husband. As I got older it seemed like I would think about my momma and sister and brother more. She never called me, nor gave me anything for my birthday or Christmas. She didn't even send for me to come to New York for summer break.

I would sometimes think "Oh my sister and brother are living in New York; they have a better life than I do. Well, I was still a child, so of course I would think that way. Who would not rather live in New York versus Wade, North Carolina?"

3
"HURTING THEN BUT DIDN'T UNDERSTAND"

I know people like to use a phrase that I just do not agree with, like saying, "No one is gonna love you like your mother." "No one is gonna treat you like your mother." Well, I say differently. Let's put on an adjective in front of Mother. And we can say, or I will say, "No one will love you like a "good" mother." "No one will treat you like a "good" mother. So, let's keep it real and be honest. If I had no one to love me and treat me better than my birth momma I guess I would have been doomed for real for real. I thank God for my grandmother, whom we called mother. She did not have much education, but she had enough love to share with eleven more children and they were not all her birth children, half of them were grandchildren like me.

Hey, let's not get it twisted, I loved my grandmother (mother), but a child would still like to have their momma in their lives. I remember my birth mother coming to North Carolina one summer; she did not bring my sister and brother. I would ask her, "Where is Cookie and Junnie?" She would say, "They are home. I could not bring them." I would later think, "Wow, they are in New York; I sure would like to go to New York to be with my sister and brother."

4
"A RING"

The only thing my momma ever gave me was this ring that she had on her finger. She said she had to get it cut off because it wouldn't come off. And I said, "When you cut it off, can I have it? "She said, "When I cut it off, I will send it to you." I said, "Ok."

Well, she did finally send the ring to me in an envelope with I guess about two paragraphs. She was never much for writing, even though she had beautiful handwriting. When I got that ring, I was so happy because my momma had given me that ring.

5
"RECORD PLAYER"

I remember another time my mom came down home. Now, I must say I have seen my birth momma about five or six times in my sixty-four years of living, as far back as I can remember. At this time, she bought me this little record player; it wasn't new but, it was something. Now, I was really in hog heaven, my momma came home and bought me a record player. I was in the eighth grade at this time. It meant a lot to me, but today's kids would probably tell their moms off. Well, she would never stay long, so she went back home to New York, and that meant I would not see her again for years and years.

By now, I'm growing up and living with my aunt RJ and uncle Jr. and their daughter Dr. Ruth. Of course, this is what we called her now, but at that time she was just a mean little girl (LOL). So, Jr. and RJ got legal custody of me and now I am their daughter too. I did not have the talks about life and stuff (guys and babies etc.). I guess I learned from school and that can be the worst teacher because you can learn stuff all the wrong way.

As I look back at my life and feel some kind of way about my birth momma, I realized that God had a plan for my life, (Jeremiah 29:11), because of things that I could have done but did not do.

6
"GOING TO HIGH SCHOOL"

Starting high school, I wanted nice clothes like other kids.

I asked my aunt if I could work in tobacco during summer break to buy my own school clothes. And of course, she said, "Yes." That was helping her as well and now she can buy just my sister's school clothes.

Well, now I'm in high school and that was a big thing to be in high school, still working during the summer in the tobacco field. That's the way a lot of children were able to buy their school clothes.

7
"HOW I MET MY HUSBAND"

Moving up into the twelfth grade, I still worked a summer job in the tobacco field. The work wasn't hard, but it was just HOT! This is where I met the man who would one day become my husband. I thought he was so handsome and fine. I just loved his walk back then, and he was left-handed, "wow." And it was a wow! Women on women"!

I was in love with this man and thinking or thought he was in love with me. His skin was so smooth and had teeth so straight, I didn't think they were real. So, as we got to know each other better I thought "Hey I'm gonna ask him if those teeth were his or were they false." One day I did ask him and yes, they were his real teeth I thought this young man was different from other guys at school. But little did I know that things were in the route to change.

We were still dating; I was never a fast girl. I thought I had someone that was so different, but little did I know, what I really had was a headache waiting to turn into a chronic migraine. He was so nice and sweet, but it didn't take too long for that all to change.

I was very naïve. Let's define *Naïve: Adj. (A person or action showing a lack of experience, wisdom, or judgment.)* That was me all the way. Just as green as a pretty fresh green lawn in the summertime. By time I was about to graduate from high school, I found out that I'm pregnant after dating for about a year. Pregnant with our first son Rell. Not knowing anything about life. I think at this point Gene knew he had a good girl and a very naive one at that. It seemed like after I got pregnant everything changed about him. He changed, but I remained the same.

He started cheating, always going out. Coming in at all different hours at night. We were young and living together. That's something that I would certainly not allow in my house. But my aunt and uncle approved it. I guess some parents think at least they know where the kids are. But nevertheless, we were doing what we called "shacking."

Hey, didn't believe in cheating, but shacking, isn't that a laugh? I often wondered why they allowed that. But anyway, Gene, began coming in later and later to not coming home at all. But he would always have a reason (a lie) why he was late or why he didn't come home. He was a very good liar, and I was very naive in believing him most of the time or rather wanting to believe him. You know it's a sad situation when you let someone have control of your life and that is what was happening to me.

When they say love is blind, well, I do know that love will cause you to see differently. It can be right in your face, and someone is telling you that it's not like that and it's not what you think. What is wrong with me?

Well, this went on for years but because I was so blind, I didn't know that he was really cheating. I just thought something wasn't right, but I still didn't know that he was really cheating. "Nita" Girl what was wrong with me? Could it be possible to be so blind? Naw! I call that stupid. Yes, I was very stupid, it took years for me to see this man didn't really love me.

One day it finally came to me that this man is playing me like a fat rat. I heard some talk around the family. It's so funny how you are always the last to know something. It seemed like the family should've told me, but instead, they just talked about it amongst each other.

8

"I PLANNED TO KILL THEM BOTH"

Well, after hearing about Gene and his playmate, I was already hurt, but was just about to lose it. I still just had my one son Rell, and Gene was nowhere in the real picture of my son and my life. Well, do you know that someone can be there, but really not there at all? This sounds like an oxymoron statement, but it's a true statement.

Trying to raise our son all by myself was not easy. But I said and I meant what I said and said what I meant. I made a mistake getting pregnant so young. But, let me say this, "I do not regret having my son." He grew up to be a very smart, AG student, academically inclined, and an "A" student, with no help from his dad of course. I promised myself that I would not have another child unless I was married and that promise I kept.

One day while being so angry and hurt after finding out that my boyfriend was having an affair with someone who was very close to me. I thought of her as being a very close and dear person in my life. I wasn't saved, so the devil was really talking to me full force. I thought of a plan that would kill them both. I figured when I got paid, I would go to one of the local pawn shops here in Fayetteville and buy a gun. It wasn't gonna be long before it was time to get paid. So, I said, "I can tell her to meet us at this secluded place not too far from where we lived." I really didn't think about the place wisely at all because that was too close to home.

But anyway, I was hurt, and I was tired of hurting. I thought to say we can all meet up and I was gonna shoot and kill them both, leaving them lying there. I was so mad. To get so mad that you will kill is not a good thing.

But, hey I thought I could kill two black people, go to prison for a few years, get out, and continue with life. I didn't think about my baby at that time. You know it's a true statement to a point that "hurt people, hurt people." If God had not intervened my life could have been doomed. And my poor baby, what was I thinking?

9
"GOD INTERVENES THROUGH A SONG"

One day while working, all I could think about was payday buying my gun to get rid of my pain renders. So, they rendered pain to me, and I was going to render some pain to them.

While working this girl began to sing this song" Because He lives, I can face tomorrow." I was so touched by that song that I told her to sing it again and every time she finished, I asked her to sing it again until I learned the song. I did not know that God was working on me at the time. God knows everything, because he knew that I was so serious. He needed to intervene, or I was about to make a shipwreck of my life and my only child at that time. I learned that song and it just blessed me to the point that I would just cry. I even cry now when I sing that song and about how God blessed me through that song. After learning the song that day, that was all I thought about for the rest of that day. God had taken the thought of killing my boyfriend and his side chick from my mind. It was as if a complete change of mind took place.

How can that happen all at once, when a few hours earlier I was excited about taking someone else's life? It was God. I praised and thanked God for stepping in at that appointed time. I still didn't know God, but at least by this time in my life, I had been to church several times and I at least knew there was a true God. Not even thinking that I could have gotten life in prison for killing those people. Thank you, Jesus!!

So, I was a little better now, at least I thought. Even though the Lord took that evil thought away. I was still hurt. I went back home after work, but still, the cheating was going on. I remember telling Gene, "I said what I meant, and I meant what I said. If you hurt me again you better hope that I'm saved or something, because if you hurt me again, I'm gonna kill you and your side chick."

He slowed down and stopped the cheating long enough to think about his life I guess, and to realize the side chick was just that and someone else's side chick as well. He cheated on me, but she had others besides him. Wow!!

So, things seemed to be going well. He decided to join the Army and that was a good thing. He went off and did his basic training. I was so happy with the change. We would talk on the phone every week. We did not have a house phone, so I had to go to the phone booth to wait for his call. He would write me letters that were long as fifteen pages. Now what he said in the letters were all about how things were going in basic training and how things were going to be different for us. And so much more, but that has been years ago, I can't remember it all.

10

"GENE COMES IN FROM BASIC TRAINING"

Well, I knew he was coming home from basic training, but he didn't tell me exactly what day. One night a taxi pulls up and I heard music playing it was him with his boombox playing the Isley Brothers... "Hello it's me." Wow! I thought that was so romantic because we had not seen each other for quite a few weeks. The boom box was the thing back in the 80s. The guys would walk around carrying their boombox. The music was much nicer and cleaner than what the young and I guess old as well listen to today. I was glad to see him, and he was glad to see us (Rell and I) as well. He only had a few weeks at home, and he would be leaving for Fort Hood, Texas. While he was home, he asked me to marry him and of course, I said, "yes." We were married on March 7th, 1980. We were happy, but wouldn't you know that the devil is always lurking anywhere he can to stir up trouble whether it's old or whatever.

When the few weeks at home were over, it was time for him to leave to go to Texas. Rell and I would meet him later after he got a place for us to live. I missed him so much and could hardly wait for him to send for us. Well, the letters would start back, and I was more ready to leave Wade, NC.

After we were married, we talked about having another child; a sister or brother for Rell. The time came for Rell and I had to leave Wade and head to Texas. I had never been to any place that far; so, I was excited about the change. We got out to Texas, and it was nice. Our lives were better, and we decided to try for another child.

I'm pregnant! We were excited about our baby. Time passes on and he was doing well in the Army. It's getting closer now to the arrival of our baby. We didn't know what it was because I'm not even sure if they were telling the genders back then. But it's almost time for delivery and Gene would be in the field a lot so he did not want me to be out in Texas alone. He asked his sister to come to stay for a little while to help me after having our baby boy TT. I had a few complications. First, he was a month early, breached and the doctor who delivered him had never delivered a baby before. They had to call in a specialist to deliver him because his feet came out first. My husband told me this later after the baby was born. My sister-in-law was saying how scared she was, but here is God stepping in again. He was fine with no problems.

We were in Texas for little over a year. My sister-in-law got married and stayed but Rell, TT and I came back with my husband. Everything was still going okay, but he ended his Army career. We stayed in Wade. Back home again, we had to start all over again. My husband started working. No matter how much I tried, it seemed like I could never get hired. It's interesting how some people who don't want to work can find a job just like that; but I could not get a job, so I stayed home with the boys. Our money was funny, our change was strange, and our credit wouldn't get it.

I was always home, and Gene always worked. This seemed all well and good, but the way things were going we both needed to work. When it looked like I was not gonna find work I stayed home. We only had one car and he would have it ninety-nine percent of the time.

11

"THINGS ARE STARTING TO CHANGE"

As time came and went, we decided to try for a baby girl. So, we did, and I was pregnant again, this time was my last time. I didn't want any more than three kids; he wanted five boys. He wanted a basketball team. I would say, "I'm not having all these kids and you walk out on me." I'm so glad that I did not listen to him about having all those kids like doorsteps.

So, now our last child is born and it's another boy. We call him DL; I was finished for good. We have our three boys Rell, TT and DL; no girls which was a part of God's plan. When you had children close back in those days people would look at you like you are crazy or something.

12

"WHEN THE REAL HURT BEGINS"

First, let us define the word *Hurt*. The dictionary says, *Hurt is a verb (an action word, it means to cause physical pain or injury to harm to wound.)* But I say hurt causes an emotional sad feeling---feeling of being betrayed, defiled, disrespected and pain.

Hurt can be an emotional, physical, and mental state of mind. There is hurt in relationship and marriages. You can ask a room full of women how many have never been hurt in their marriage or relationship raise your hand. And if they can be honest, there will not be many (just a few) that will raise their hand. I did say" emotionally physically and mentally."

It takes the Lord to take away the hurt. My hurt came in my marriage. I was young and in love with my husband like any other wife. I was very faithful, I believe that if you are married you should only give your body to your husband, if you are a woman. If you are a man, you should only give your body to your wife. This is the way

God designed it to be. I did not and still do not believe in cheating. He was and still is the only man that I have given my body to. I don't know where all this faithfulness came from because I certainly did not learn it in church.

I did not see, nor did I know that the road that I was traveling on would be so long and bumpy with so much pain. But this is the plan God had for me. I can remember so many times asking God, "Why am I going through this? I'm a pretty good lady, I have my three sons I'm trying to raise. I don't cheat on my husband and don't want to cheat, Lord why? It hurts Lord! Why?"

The hurt was beginning again but this time he is my husband and I'm his wife, it's no boyfriend-girlfriend thing. It's the real thing this time. The Lord was beginning to let me know that it was part of the plan He had for me. But I really did not like that plan, but in the end, it would yield the peaceable fruit (Heb. 12:11).

Well, I didn't know about that but, later I found out it was so. I did not know that the hurt would last two decades and some. My word! I was hurt in so many ways by the man who said he loved me and married me. The man changed so fast, that I did not have time to regroup or get myself in order, so I thought. I met this Christian lady during a bus driver training, and she introduced me to her Pastor and First Lady, who happened to be her sister. I thank God for meeting this lady because through this lady, and the Pastor & First Lady, I met an amazing man who loved me in spite of all the devilish things I had on my mind. I once had on my mind. His name is above every name. His name is Jesus. After meeting the Pastor and the First Lady, they invited me to church. I did not own any dresses or skirts but just had one dress. I remember that was an old ugly beige dress. I told them I would go to church, but they would have to pick me up. They were happy to come by to get my boys and me.

Gene would not come to church, at this time because he was really getting back out there. The First Lady came by to pick us up on that Sunday; We started going to church. I actually enjoyed the church service. The church attendance was very small, but it was okay. They didn't have a choir, so after going to church for a while, they put together a choir.

This was in 1983. My boys ages at the time; Rell was turning six TT was a two and D.L had just turned one in May. So, I had babies. I went to church every Sunday with my boys. But one Sunday I felt like I needed more than just going to church. I needed a personal relationship with God. I felt like I had no one to talk to, I needed

Jesus in my heart. So, I decided to make the first real step towards this relationship with Jesus. I got baptized in the name of our Lord Jesus Christ. Well, that's not the first step--let me back up. The first step is to truly repent of all your sins, then comes the baptism in the name of Jesus. I got baptized on February 6th, 1984. I thought that was all I needed, and I was good. But there was one more step that was very important.

We (the church family) were invited to a church in Fayetteville, NC where our Pastor had to speak, and we (the church) would always go for support. While at the church service this lady got up and had words after the preaching and she said, "You are not saved if you do not have the Holy Ghost."

My sister-in-law and I were very upset about that, because we thought for sure we were heaven bound. When we got a chance to speak to our First Lady about what the lady had said. Our First Lady answered, "You are not completely saved until you receive the Holy Ghost with the evidence of speaking in tongues," (Acts 2:4). Well, we were like what do we do? We had been getting good teaching, but we were babies in Christ and did not understand all that. I'm so glad she told us. Because we needed that "keeping power." That same power the raised Jesus from the grave was the same power we needed in our life. We began to desire and want that power. It's yours for the asking but you have to really want the Holy Ghost.

When you get serious about serving God, you will do whatever to get the Holy Ghost. Which is repenting seriously and to stop all of what you can stop doing(sinning). We know that there are some things you just cannot do for yourself. That is why we have a good and loving God named Jesus. My husband is still cutting up, and I felt like I really needed the Holy Ghost in my life at this time. I needed Jesus Spirit living in my heart. I was tired of the infidelity, it seemed like my entire relationship was a mess.

The summer of August 1985, I had a great hunger for the Spirit of God. I wanted the Holy Ghost, and I needed the Holy Ghost. I loved wearing pants and big earrings but not as big as they wear now. I just thought I'd never give that up. But, let me tell you something, when you are serious, and you want something bad enough you will give up and do whatever you feel like it takes. I gave up something that I loved to get something that I needed, which was the Holy Ghost. It seemed like almost every Sunday at church I would just be touched by the Spirit of God, and I would just cry out all the time and would be on the floor every time I would go up to the altar for prayer. Crying out to Jesus because He was the only one that knew my heart and pain. I was so depressed at times but trying to hold it together.

But do you know it's hard trying to hold it all together, when it feels like everything at home is falling apart. I was not the best singer, but I would sing songs that would minister to me. Such as, *"Because He lives, I Can Face Tomorrow,"* *"Send It On Down Lord, Lord Let The Holy Ghost Come On Down,"* and so, so many more. And it seemed like every time I would sing, *"He Keeps on Making a Way for Me,"* by a Gospel group named, The Truthettes, I loved their songs and *"God Will Make Things Alright."* Songs like those are needed more now. There are not as many songs that minister to the hurting soul these days. Those songs really helped along with my praying and fasting. Jesus saw me in my hurt and pain, and he knew that one day (but not that day) he was going to stop the hurt from hurting. My God! Hallelujah!!

Sometimes I did not want to go up for prayer, but I knew that I needed it. I knew when I got up to the altar, as soon as Pastor would lay hands, (I was already hurting and crying to the Lord for help) next thing I knew I would just see feet because I'm on the floor again. I needed that touch from God because I knew when I got home, I had to face the enemy. At this time, I did not work. My husband was the only provider so what he didn't buy we just did not have. He was concerned about his feeling good juice of beer and smoking pot. That was never a part of my life. I grew up with people drinking all around me, but I never desired any of that stuff. God had a plan for me.

So, I was growing just a little bit in Christ, but was not strong enough to stand against the wiles of the devil. The First Lady would tell me to ask Gene to come to church. I would ask him, but only later in the week. He would say, "I wish you would stop asking me to go to church, when I'm ready I will."

So, when first lady would ask if I asked him, I would tell her exactly what he said. She would say something like, "It's all right, he's coming." I would think, well she knows more than I, because that man had a stubborn spirit. He told me, "I'm not going to change, I was born a Baptist and I'm gonna die a Baptist." I didn't care whether he was a Baptist or Pentecostal Holiness or Apostolic Holiness I just wanted him saved and to stop cheating. As I was saying, it was a hot, hot summer in August 1985, I wanted the Holy Ghost so bad that I went on a fast for three and a half days and three nights with no food just water. I worked in tobacco field during that summer. It was as hot as fish grease out there, (My sister likes to say that). But-- God, it was all God, who saw that my heart was ready to receive his precious gift.

13
"RECEIVING THAT PRECIOUS GIFT OF THE HOLY GHOST"

One Sunday a few weeks later at church, the sister who played the piano and in charge of the choir, asked me to sing this particular song. She said, "I prayed and asked the Lord what to sing," Well, I really didn't want to sing, and she said, "Out of obedience, sing it, please." Out of obedience, I sang the song, *"Lord Send It On Down, Lord Let The Holy Ghost Come On Down."*

Well, I began to lead this song and our little choir was singing and backing me up. I don't know what happened between "Lord *I Can't Smile, and I Can't Live Right Until You Send It Down,*" but, when I came to myself, I was on the floor waddling over the floor and "speaking in tongues." I heard myself speaking. But we were taught that you have to know you received for yourself. No one would tell you that you received the Holy Ghost.

I remember feeling so good when I got up off the floor and went home, even though I knew nothing had changed in my home, but now I had the POWER to keep me and I still cried, but I was stronger now, for a while anyway. But don't you know the devil was mad because he lost one of his warriors--me).

So, the hurt was still hurting. Sometimes I could feel the other church family feeling sorry for me, saying, "Here is sister McLucas and her three boys, she is faithful though." I learned if you be faithful to God, he will be faithful to you. My whole marriage was about cheating. I had more cheating/bad days than good days, but the weight of the good days outweighed all of the bad days.

It was like having three rolls of paper towels on the left and they are dry and having three rolls of paper towels on the right and they are soaking wet, so then the weight of the wet paper towels on the right is heavier. So, that is how my marriage was, I had more bad days than good days, but the few good days outweighed the bad days.

I still prayed and fasted, believing that one-day things will be different. When you hear of emotional, mental, and physical abuse, it is real.

So let me break down these three words that were a part of my life for real. Emotionally, it began to make me feel like I was less than a woman. I thought I was what my husband wanted, and I guess at one time I was. But the devil was putting his hands all in our lives.

When you love someone and, it seems that they don't love you back... What do you do?

You HURT! HURT! HURT!

Mentally, the hurt and pain of being rejected disrespected and being treated like all I did was not good enough, was beginning to play with my mind because I still love my husband. That's why I stayed at the altar.

What do you do when your spouse has found someone else to replace you?

You HURT! HURT! HURT!

Physically, I didn't have any physical pain. He was not the kind of man that would hit me. I'm glad that was not in him. I know I could not stop him from cheating but believe me when I say, "I say what I mean, and I mean what I say," I could STOP him if he was a hitter. He had to sleep some time. The only person I know who never sleeps is Jesus. He doesn't sleep nor slumber. But man (humans) must sleep sometime.

How do you deal with so much and have a God on your side, but do not know him? Those were the times that I just cried, cried, and cried. You see I did not know Him as a deliverer yet. So, all I knew was to be faithful, pray cry if I must, and keep going as best that I could. Just crying and calling on a God that I did not know yet. Sometimes we call on God when we are in trouble and need him but after he has done the thing you want from him, we just forget him and cast him to the side.

I was broken but did not know how to fix it. Have you ever broken something but didn't know how to fix it? Well, I didn't know how to fix our relationship. How many of you know that just because you serve God and do your best, we are not exempt from hurt and pain? I learned through all of this pain of infidelity, disrespect, lying, mistrust, and distrust that God is still bigger and greater than anything I could or will go through.

I can remember so many times I would be on my knees praying and crying to God, and one of the boys would come in the room. When they would come in or knock on the door they would say, "Momma are you praying?" I would reply, "Yes I'll be in there in a few minutes." That was how I made it through, by praying and reading my Bible.

I was in this *serving God until I die mode*. I had no one else, but so many saints and sinners would encourage me that God is going to bless you. Some would say, "You keep on serving the Lord, he is going to bless you."

My husband would seem to do better for a little while and promises that he was finished with that. But really how long did he keep that promise?

Now when I look back at all the stuff, I went through with him and wonder why did I take all that? One time I tried looking for a place for me and the boys. I found this house, called, and the man on the other end asked, "How many were in the family?" I said, "four." He said, "The place was not big enough." I think he recognized my voice sounded like a black lady. So, that was out, I didn't have money anyway, I guess I was reaching for a miracle. I didn't tell Gene I was trying to leave. I think he probably didn't care anyway. This man was just a crazy mad man, he had a good wife and kids but that wasn't good enough. Sometimes we did not see Gene for about three or four days.

14

"THINGS WERE LOOKING A LITTLE BETTER"

I took the bus driver's test and got my CDLs, and the Lord bless me to get a bus driving job at one of the local schools where my boys attended. It was good for me to get to school, but I had to get back home from school, having no car, I would walk about a mile and a half from my house to the main highway in the afternoon to catch another bus that was going to the school that I drove at, I had gotten permission from the principal that the bus driver could pick me up in the afternoon and drop me off in the morning. It was a long walk, but I did what I had to do. Gene had a car, but he drove it to work, so that left me to fend for myself. This went on for about one week, I think. And one day I saw my First Lady at school, she worked there, I cannot remember for sure, but I don't think I asked her, but I think she offered, that I could drive her car home so I would have a ride back in the evening, I was SO GRATEFUL!!

So, God was moving me in the direction, he had for me to go. Just let me say this, "God is a jealous God." He said, "He will have no other god before him." Sometimes we don't even notice that we have made our spouse, our children, our jobs or anything else, a god. GOD DOES NOT like that. That's what I had done with my husband. I was so in love with this man, that I was blind to all his tactics. So, when we put anything or anyone before God, he will allow it to take wings and fly away. Now, you understand not really take wings, but they will definitely walk away. Ladies, DON'T DO IT!

Don't make your children your god. Sure, love them but if you make a god of them and I promise you that nine times out of ten they will disappoint you.

15

"I PAID MY TITHES"

Now I have a ride back home in the morning and a ride back to school in the afternoon. I didn't have money to pay my First Lady, so she understood. Back in those days, in the late 1980s you certainly did not bring home much from a bus driver's paycheck. I don't like to say nothing because I believe that something is better than zero. when I was home, I was making zero. So, this little bit was better than zero. I remember my bus number was 356 and I brought home around $386 a month.

Some may say, "That's nothing," but when you had nothing, you will appreciate that $386. I would give my First Lady about $20 for letting me use her car and burn her gas. She didn't ask for anything, but I knew gas wasn't free. She was such a blessing in my time of need.

But I want you all to know, I paid my tithe out of that $386. God had a long lesson for me to learn and it seemed to have taken a long time to learn it. The same as if you don't pass your grade in school, you have to repeat it, and that's the way I was.

So, I worked driving the bus in 1986 and continued paying my tithes. One day Gene brought a 1975 Nova that was his car, just like all the others were his. I think I may have driven that car once or twice and that was only if he was at home and not going anywhere. But I still had a ride back home and back to the bus. God is so good. So, I had two of my boys in school and the baby boy would spend the entire week at my mother-in-law and father-in-law's house because I did not have transportation to take him back and forth to their house every day, it was too far and too much anyway.

They were a blessing to me as well during my dark days. DL liked staying with his granddaddy and grandmomma, and she really loved having him there, that was company for her when our daddy was working. I would get a ride to pick him up on Fridays.

So, this went on for a while. My father-in-law and mother-in-law were great. I know some people have serious issues with their in-laws, well, I've never had any issues with mine. My sisters-in-law felt like a sister to me, closer than my biological sister. My brothers-in-law were the same to me, like brothers. And of course, their wives and their sister's husbands.

16

"THANKFUL FOR MY CHURCH FAMILY"

One day I was going to my First Lady's house, she was gonna do my hair and Gene had let me use the car to get my hair fixed. I saw this truck following me, I'm wondering why is this truck following me. When I pulled up in the yard of the Pastor and First Lady the truck followed me all the way there. The man got out of the truck and said, "Ma'am I'm sorry, but I have to pick up this car. There has not been a payment made since it was bought." I was so embarrassed, but it could have happened at a store or somewhere else, so I guess God allowed it to be at that time. My First Lady saw it all and I was so embarrassed. Even though he took the car, I watched God work through this embarrassment. Later, when I got home, Gene had gotten a ride home and I told him the car lot people came and repossessed the car, he acted surprised. I told him, "The man said you haven't made any payments." Now listen to this, he replied, "What?" I made a car payment." Wow!! He still got it, can lie with a straight face. I said, "What are you gonna do?" He said, "I ain't going to do nothing, I reckon they can keep it then." I was like, "If you made a payment, you should say something." He said, "I ain't worried about that Nita."

That was that. Later the First Lady asked about the car and what was he going to do about it, I told her what he had said. And she said, "Call the car lot and ask if you can take over the payments. I did that and had to do all the paperwork over. Now this car was mine and in my name. Gene didn't come home that night or that weekend. I drove the car back home, because they filled the car up with gas before I left. I was so happy. He hardly would let me use his lil' car, but now I owned his (what was his) lil' car!

When he finally came home, BOY! Was he surprised. "Where did you get the car from? I thought they took it?" he said. I replied, "They did, but I bought it back." Man, you could have bought him for one penny, that is how cheap he looked. "Where did you get the money from?" He wanted to know. The Lord had touched the heart of the Pastor, First Lady, and another sister in the church to bless me with enough money to get it back. I didn't tell him where the money came from because that was none of his business.

17

"GOD WILL DELIVER, EVENTUALLY"

Well, y'all the hurt is still hurting, but God is about to release me just for a little while. I still had much more to go through. If you want to know when the hurt stopped hurting, you will have to follow the hurt to the next edition.

This is not a fairy tale; it was my reality……

The true story of my life.

The second edition is coming soon. God took the hurt out of the hurt!!!

Keep watching for my second edition. I pray that my story has and will help you ladies that may have or may be going through a situation like this one or similar.

God did deliver, but you will have to read the next edition, to see how God did it.

God will deliver!

Don't tell me that God won't deliver, I know he will. I am a witness that God will deliver on time.

I give All the Glory and Honor to God through all my trials, God has made me strong, I thank God for the Holy Ghost that kept me, and today my life has changed. I am no longer the same naive little lady. God put a power in me that I needed and today I am so Grateful. He has delivered and set free. So don't tell me that God won't deliver, I know he will. There is a time and season for everything, your season of deliverance is coming. You may be hurt, but you can cope with it, when God has a plan for you. He is there with you, through it all. Believe me when I thought I could not make it, God would give me that extra boost of energy and faith.

Being hurt by your boyfriend or husband is not something that we want anyone to know while going through, but just wait and trust God, because he is the only one you can truly trust to see you through, in Jesus' name!

Ways to contact Author Inita McLucas

Email address: Initamclucas06@gmail.com

Telephone number: (910) 797-7151

Made in the USA
Middletown, DE
18 September 2023